The Spider Club

by Alice Cary
illustrated by Diane Blasius

Open Court Publishing Company
Chicago and Peru, Illinois

Printed in the United States of America

ISBN 0-8126-1279-5

10 9 8 7 6 5 4 3

"Run, Grace!" yelled Mike. "It's a spider!"

"Run?" said Grace. "What for?"

"Girls hate spiders," said Mike.

"Not me," said Grace. "I like spiders.
My sister and I have a spider club."

4

"That is a garden spider," said Grace.
"It has eight eyes!"

"It has lots of legs, too," said Mike.

"Yes, all spiders have eight legs," said Grace.

"Are all spiders alike?" asked Mike.

Grace led Mike to the Spider Club.
Inside the club were lots of spiders.

"No, not all spiders are alike," Grace said.

6

"Here is a spider that jumps," said Grace.

"Jumps? Yikes!" said Mike.

"Not on you," said Grace. "It jumps on insects."

"Can't it spin a web?" asked Mike.

"No," said Grace, "not all spiders spin webs."

"This spider makes a trap, not a web," said Grace.
"It digs a trap and hides in it.
Insects fall into the trap."

"Which spider do you like best?" asked Mike.

8

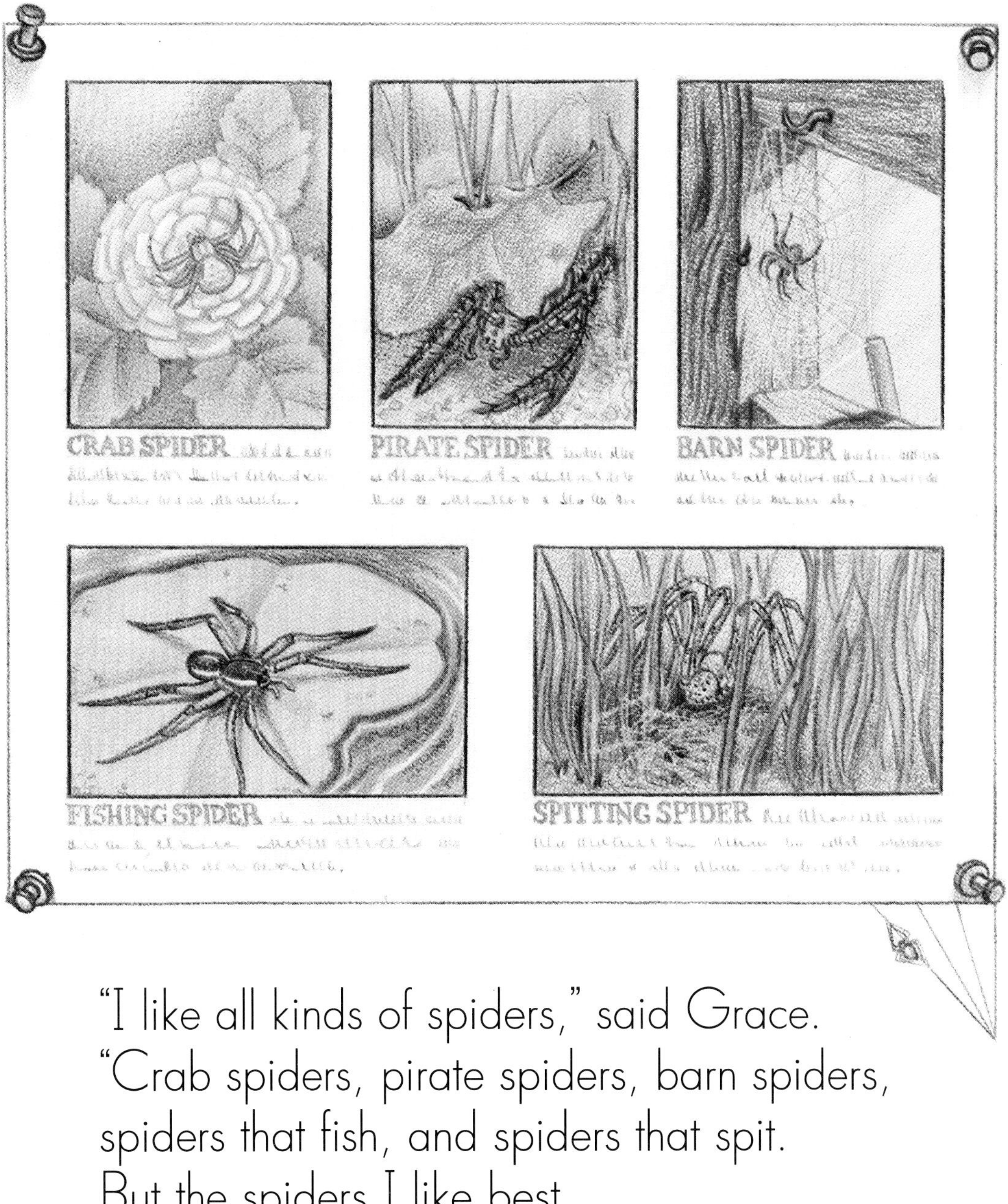

"I like all kinds of spiders," said Grace.
"Crab spiders, pirate spiders, barn spiders,
spiders that fish, and spiders that spit.
But the spiders I like best
are the ones that spin webs.
I bet we can find one outside."

"Here's a spider!" called Mike.
"Will it spin a web?"

"Sit still," said Grace, "and we will find out."

"Oh! It fell from the branch!" yelled Mike.
"It made a thread!"

"That thread is made of silk," said Grace.

"Isn't silk for shirts?" asked Mike.

"Not spider silk," said Grace.

"A spider makes two kinds of silk.
One kind sticks to things," said Grace.
"When an insect hits the web,
it sticks to the silk."

"This silk thread is called a dragline.
The spider rides on the end of it.
Then the spider makes two bridges."

"What a trick!" said Mike.

"What next?" asked Mike.

"The spider runs from bridge to bridge," said Grace. "It spins and spins to make a frame for the web."

14

"Next, it fills in the frame," said Grace.
"It spins fast."

"What a wonderful web!" said Mike.
"What will it do next?"

"It's time to dine," said Grace.
"The spider will sit still
until an insect hits the web.
It wants a nice snack."

"Me too!" said Mike. "It's time for lunch!"